Explore M

MUTASIA®: Land of Illogical & Utterly Impossible Critters

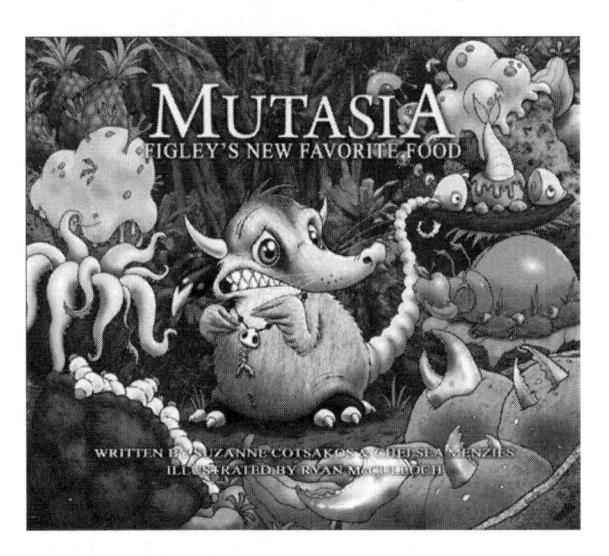

MUTASIA®: Figley's New Favorite Food

FIGLEY'S ADVENTURES CONTINUE IN...

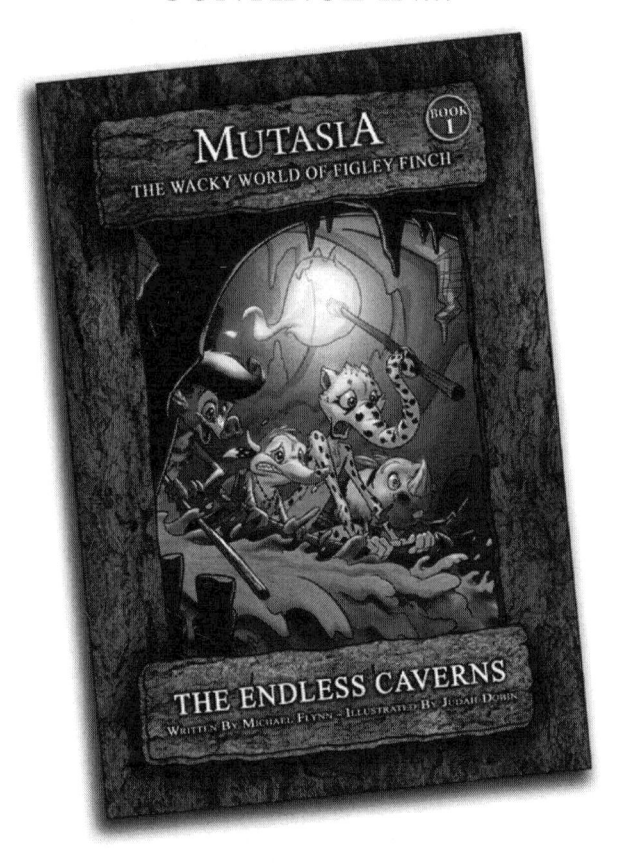

THE
ENDLESS CAVERNS

Mutasia®: The Wacky World of Figley Finch

Book 2

"Clubhouse Clash"

Written by Justin Minkel
Illustrated by Judah Dobin

A Mutasian Entertainment, LLC Publication

Written by:
Justin Minkel

Illustrated by:
Judah Dobin

Creative Concepts by:
Tami Cotsakos
Suzanne Cotsakos
Ryan McCulloch
Chelsea Menzies

Special Thanks to Joseph Fatheree & Brigitte VanBaelen

Published by Mutasian Entertainment, LLC

Printed in the U.S.A.

MUTASIA® is a registered trademark of Mutasian Media, LLC
Copyright © 2012-2013 by Mutasian Media, LLC
All rights reserved, including the right of reproduction in whole or in part in any form.

Discover Mutasia's books, apps, music and more at:
www.mutasia.com

ISBN: 978-0-9856002-1-1
LCCN: 2012943765

First Edition

This book is dedicated to the children and grown-ups at Jones Elementary. You make Jones a magical place to teach and learn.

This book is also dedicated to my daughter, Ariana, who laughs every time she hears nibs sing.

Owen Hunter,
I hope you like this adventure!

— Justin

CONTENTS

1.	Larva Cake	1
2.	Wrong Song	9
3.	The Tough Guys' Clubhouse vs. The Fierce Females' Fort	17
4.	War!	29
5.	Caught in the Crossfire	37
6.	Stung Tongue	45
7.	Peace Talk	51
Epilogue: The Feast		55

MUTASIA®
THE WACKY WORLD OF FIGLEY FINCH
CLUBHOUSE CLASH

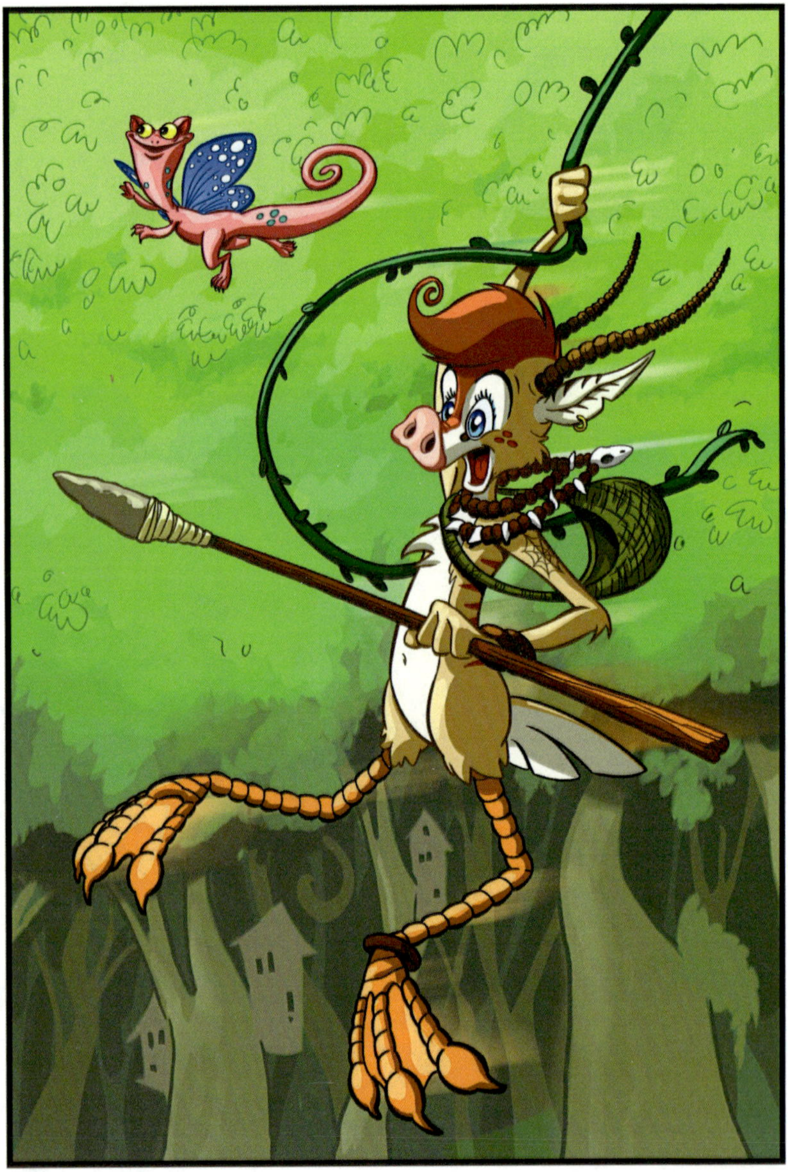

Chapter One: Larva Cake

The sun rose red over Tree Village. Sunlight spilled through the branches, lighting up the huts that clung to the huge trees. Zabetta stepped out onto the deck of her tree house. Her spear dangled from one hand, and she cradled a jug of mingo milk in her arm. She took a long swallow of the murky milk. Then she corked the jug and wrapped her fingers in a vine dangling beside her deck. A winged meowzer drifted past, its polka-dotted wings cupped to catch the breeze.

"Today's my friend Figley's half-birthday,"

Zabetta told the meowzer. "I'm going hunting for the secret ingredient in his favorite kind of cake." The meowzer perched on the vine and flicked out its curly tongue at her.

Zabetta laughed. Sunrise was her favorite time for hunting in Tree Village. The breeze was cool, but not cold. Steam rose like a sea of clouds from the damp ground far below. She took a tight grip on the vine and sprang off the platform.

She whooshed through the air, the wind ruffling her fur and feathers. "Yahooooo!" she shouted. She let go of the vine, turned a flip in the air, and grabbed a new vine. Soon she saw what she was looking for—a grove of yackle trees. The black branches bent in zig-zags. Huge papery hives dangled like bright blue piñatas from every branch.

"Here goes," she whispered. She wrapped one leg in the vine and swung toward the biggest hive. She pulled back the spear like a baseball bat.

Whack! She smashed a ragged hole in the side of the hive. A growling buzz started up right away. Six bright insects crawled out of the hole, their armor gleaming like metal. They were venomous waspitoes, each with a deadly stinger on its rear end and a long needle nose. The waspitoes' wings vibrated. Their needle noses quivered as bright black drops of venom beaded on the tips.

Zabetta took a deep breath as her vine swung back toward the buzzing hive. The waspitoes lifted into the air and zoomed toward her, swift and sharp as darts. She slashed left and right with her spear, cutting the waspitoes into pieces before they got the chance to sting her. Scraps of waspito wings drifted down like confetti.

"Adiós, waspitoes!" Zabetta shouted, smiling a fierce grin. She swung back toward the smashed hive and hooked her foot in a branch. She took a spoon made of droolly hammoth bone from the hunting bag slung over her shoulder. She dipped the spoon into the hive and scooped up a big spoonful of the gray waspito larvae huddled at the bottom. Then she scraped the slimy larvae into a stone jar.

"Delicious," she said, smiling down at the squirming gray larvae. "Figley's going to love this larva cake!"

Zabetta climbed down the branches until she reached the forest floor. She ran through the forest, zig-zagging around the huge tree trunks in her path and leaping over a patch of sink-sand, until she reached a field of bright orange and pink blossoms. She took a deep breath of the flowers' fragrant scent. "Snapping myrtle," she said. "They smell so sweet you'd never know their favorite food is Mutasians."

She slid down the vine and landed in front of a four-foot, carnivorous flower. Its bright orange blossoms were folded tight. She lifted her spear and tickled the top of the blossom. The flower lunged at her. The petals peeled back like lips, and a greenish beak snapped shut on the end of her spear. "Nice try," Zabetta told the flower. She pulled a flint knife from her bag and cut off a few petals. "These will be perfect for decorating Figley's cake," she told the flower. "Thanks!"

She yanked her spear free of the snapping myrtle's beak. Then she climbed the nearest vine and swung toward home to bake her cake. She was feeling so happy about Figley's half-birthday surprise, she started to sing. "Oh, Figley's my jiggly buddy, he has such a squiggly tail, he's round and he's furry, and I never worry, because he's my number-one pal!"

As she swung, she noticed a big snapping myrtle blossom thrash back and forth, spitting long strands of nectar on the other flowers. Zabetta stopped singing, loosened her grip, and dropped to the jungle floor. She tip-toed toward the flower with her spear raised.

A big fuzzy rump with a beaver tail stuck out of the flower's beak. Zabetta knew that rump. "Rhumbler!" she shouted. "Hold on—I'll get you out!" She jabbed her spear into the beak. She pulled on one end with all her weight, and her friend Rhumbler popped out.

"Oh, thank you, Zabetta, thank you!" Rhumbler's rhino horn was covered with pink pollen. Her chubby body was shaking with fright. "I was pollinating the snapping myrtles," she said, "being really careful not to get snapped, when I heard you coming. I looked up, and then..." She pointed at the pink nectar smeared all over her stripes.

"No problem," Zabetta told her. "Hey, if you see Wattee and Chadwick, tell them we're going to throw a surprise half-birthday party for Figley at his hut. I'm going home to make his cake."

Zabetta climbed the nearest tree, grabbed a vine, and swung off toward home. Rhumbler buzzed off to find her friends, with Zabetta's new song stuck in her head.

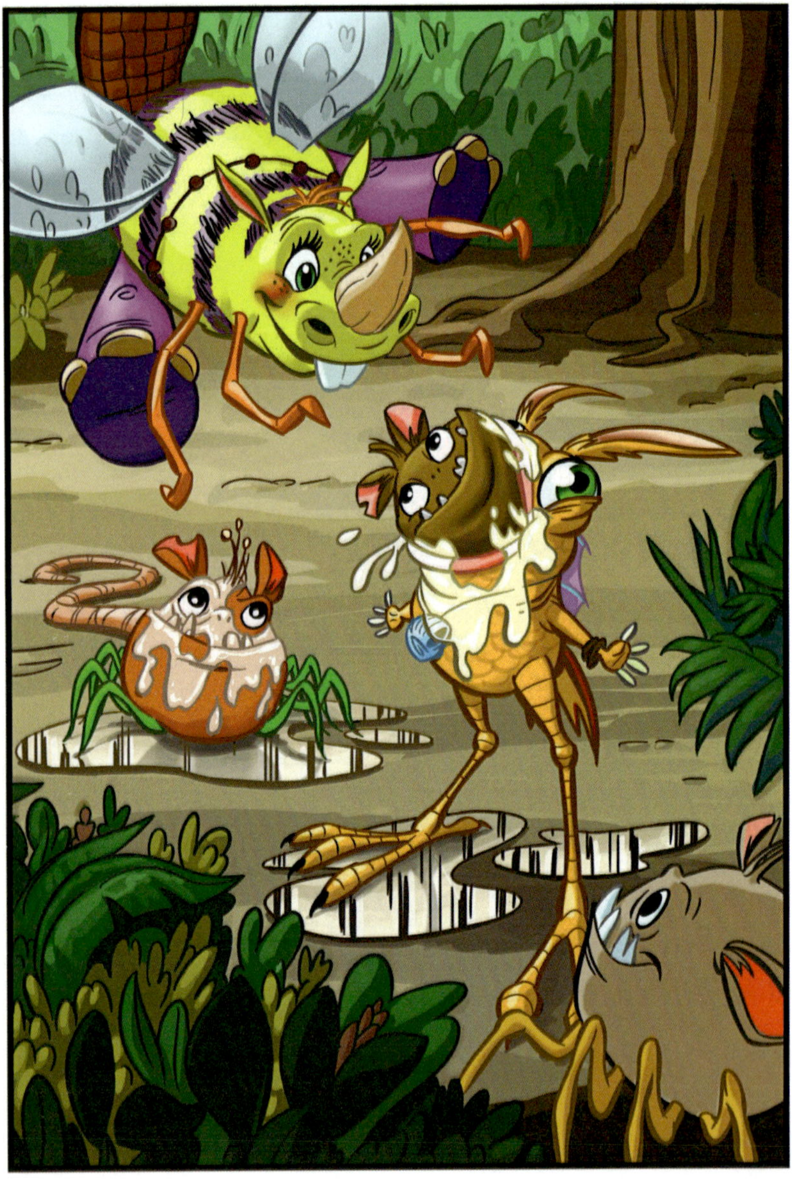

Chapter Two: Wrong Song

Rhumbler found Wattee having a nib-spitting contest with himself. His scaled cheeks were puffed wide, and drool ran down his chin. He hopped in the air and spat the chuckling nib as far as he could.

Rhumbler buzzed over, still singing Zabetta's song about Figley. She hadn't heard the words clearly when she was stuck in the snapping myrtle blossom, but she thought she remembered most of them. "Oh, Figley's my piggiest buddy, he has such a silly bald tail, he's round and he's chubby, his belly's so tubby, because he's my bumble-tum pal!"

Wattee glared at her. He picked up the nib, its white fur stuck up in wet spikes, and stuffed it back into his mouth. "What are you singing about?" he mumbled.

"It's a song Zabetta made up about Figley," she told him. "We're having a party for his half-birthday. Make sure he's home around lunchtime, and we'll come surprise him, OK?"

"If I feel like it," Wattee said.

"Whatever." Rhumbler buzzed back into the air. "Have you seen Chadwick?"

"He's gone for the day," Wattee said. "Probably collecting dirt samples or something."

Wattee hopped toward the river, singing the song he thought he'd heard. "Oh, Figley's my stinkiest buddy, he has such a goofy bald tail, he's fat and he's smelly, like stenchaloupe jelly, he's so weird we should put him in jail!"

He shook his head. "Man, that's a mean song," he said. "Doesn't sound like something Zabetta would sing." He stopped and gasped. "She must be mad at Figley. I bet the party's a trick! She's probably going to poison him or something— oh, no!" He ran off as fast as his chicken legs could carry him, hurrying to warn Figley about the trap.

Meanwhile, at the edge of the Squonk Valley

River, Figley was perched on a little rock. He wiggled his feet in the water, watching his fishing pole. For bait, he had hooked an old boot filled with rotten stenchaloupe melons to the end of the line. When the tip of the boot jerked under the water, Figley shrieked with delight. He grabbed the pole with his tail, picked up his net, and lunged toward the water. He hauled out a huge furry fish. Its wet body twisted and thrashed in the net. Thwap! Its flat tail thumped Figley in the head, and he tumbled into the water. The fish swam away down the river, dragging his net with it.

Figley crawled out onto the muddy bank, coughing up river water. Wattee was waiting for him. Wattee sucked in a deep breath and said in a rush, "Rhumbler said Zabetta said a bunch of mean stuff about you, like you're stinky and your tail's goofy, and she's coming over later today with a poisonous cake to trick you for your half-birthday!"

Figley smiled. "She remembered my half-birthday?"

Wattee groaned. "Didn't you hear me? She sang this song about you, like you have a bald tail and everything."

Figley picked up his pink tail. "It *is* bald," he pointed out.

Wattee shook his head. "Listen to the song." He cleared his throat and sang, "Oh, Figley's my stinkiest buddy, he has such a goofy bald tail, he's fat and he's smelly, like stenchaloupe jelly, he's so weird we should put him in jail!"

Figley stopped smiling. He sniffed at the boot full of soggy stenchaloupe. Then he sniffed his armpits. "That's mean," he said. "Maybe I should go talk to her, and find out why she—"

Wattee pushed Figley in the chest so hard he fell down. "We're tough guys in Tree Village, not sissies! If you're that much of a wimp, I don't want to be your friend. And when I tell Chadwick, he won't either."

Figley got to his feet. "Okay, Wattee. I'll do whatever you say, if you'll keep on being my friend."

Wattee grinned and slapped him on the

shoulder. "I knew you were a tough guy. Now, we're going to need that stinky boot, a dozen nibs, and a whole bunch of fishhooks."

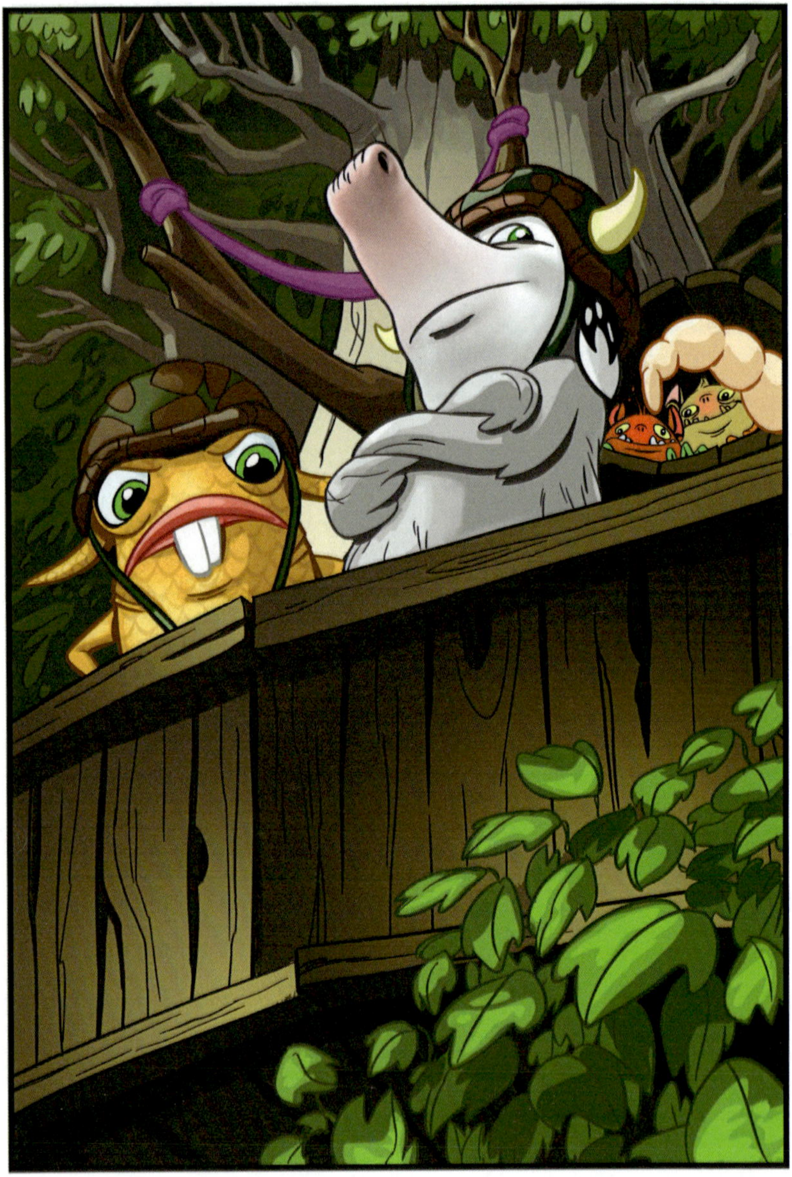

Chapter Three: The Tough Guys' Clubhouse vs. The Fierce Females' Fort

By lunchtime, Figley's hut looked like a war zone. Gleaming fishhooks were scattered all over the porch. Figley and Wattee crouched on the roof in a fort built of branches. Their faces were streaked with war paint, and they wore gortuga shells on their heads as helmets. They had made a huge slingshot from a six-foot strip of droolly hammoth gut and a Y-shaped branch that grew out of the roof. The boot of stenchaloupe stood beside a wooden barrel full of puffy white nibs who were chirping and hopping with joy. A plank of wood was nailed across the hut's doorway, with big black words that Wattee had written in river mud: "Tough Guys' Clubhouse—Girls Keep Out (Especially If Your Name Is Zabetta Or Rhumbler!)" Beneath those words, Figley had added a PS: "Yor tal iz goofyr then myn, Zabetta!"

 Figley and Wattee didn't have to wait long. As the sun rose toward noon, they heard Zabetta's "Yahooooo!" She swung from vine to vine, holding a huge gray cake under one arm. Rhumbler buzzed along behind her. She was humming the song about Figley.

 "I told you," Wattee said. He whacked Figley on his helmet. "See the cake? Hear the song? They're coming to poison you!"

 Zabetta swung up onto the porch and let go of the vine. She landed on a tangle of fishhooks with both feet. "Owwwwwww!" she shouted. She dropped the cake, and it smashed all over the porch. Squishy waspito larvae started squirming out of the frosting. Zabetta sat down to pull the fishhooks out of her webbed feet, but she sat right on another tangle of fishhooks. "Owwwwwww!" she howled again. She jumped up in the air, holding her feathered bottom in both hands.

Rhumbler buzzed over and started untangling the fishhooks from Zabetta's feet. She stopped when she noticed the sign across the doorway. Her mouth fell open. "Zabetta, look! Those slimy, scaly, bald-tailed little magglerats!"

"Watch who you're calling names, Dumbler!" Wattee said. He leaned over the roof to look down at her.

Rhumbler's eyes filled with tears. "We shouldn't have even invited you to the party, Snotty Wattee!"

Wattee grabbed a nib from the barrel. He dunked it in the boot of rotten stenchaloupe, and stuck it in the slingshot's pouch. Whap! The nib caught Rhumbler right in her front teeth. She charged Wattee, lowered her horn, and rammed him in the belly. Wattee tumbled backward off the roof and thumped on the back porch.

Figley grabbed a nib, dunked it in the boot, and loaded the slingshot. But Rhumbler was already retreating, gagging and choking on the mouthful of stenchaloupe. Zabetta swung from vine to vine beside her. She looked furious.

Wattee climbed the ladder from the back porch to the roof. He flopped down beside Figley, still breathing hard from his fall. "We showed them, buddy," he wheezed. "They won't mess with The Tough Guys again!"

Figley shook his head. "We shouldn't have done it." He yanked the lid off the barrel of nibs.

The nibs scurried away, squeaking and chirping, and hopped off the roof.

"Oh, yeah?" Wattee said. He grabbed Figley by the tail and dragged him to the edge of the roof. "Look." The nibs were devouring the smashed cake on the porch. Their tiny teeth gnashed as they gobbled down the larvae and licked up the frosting. "Those greedy little nibs just ate a poisonous cake," Wattee said. "Watch—they're all going to get sick."

Figley and Wattee watched as the nibs finished off the cake. Their bellies were rounder than before, but they seemed fine. They hopped off the porch and skittered down the vines, still squeaking cheerfully.

"Umm," Wattee said. "I guess they, I mean, I guess the poison doesn't hurt nibs—but if *you* had eaten the cake..."

"No way, Wattee," Figley said. "I'm going to find Rhumbler and Zabetta to tell them I'm sorry."

Wattee grabbed his arm. "You take one step off this porch, and you're banned from the clubhouse forever!"

"Umm, it's my house," Figley reminded him.

"Oh, yeah," said Wattee. He scratched his head. "I'm going to make a new clubhouse, then." He stomped to the other end of the porch, grabbed a vine, and slid down it. Figley climbed up the tree and took the first branch toward Zabetta's hut. A guilty feeling filled his stomach, as if he had swallowed a stone. He took a deep breath and went to tell his friends he was sorry.

By the time Figley arrived at Zabetta's hut, he didn't recognize it. Waspito hives hung from every branch. Zabetta had potted a row of snapping myrtle blossoms along the front porch. She sat on the roof beside a large fire, sharpening a pile of arrows with a flint knife.

Figley gulped. "Zabetta!" he squeaked. "It's

Figley. I came to talk to you."

Zabetta scowled and slammed her knife blade into the wooden roof. She held up one of her duck feet. It was bandaged with a slimy green plant. "You see this, Figley? I have six holes in my foot from those fishhooks." She picked up her bow and notched an arrow to the string. Figley started scrambling back down the vine headfirst. "Remember that nasty stenchaloupe your pal

Wattee shot at Rhumbler's face? Well, she was still gagging when we got back." Zabetta dipped the arrowhead in the fire, and the tip lit up like a torch. Figley kept scrambling down. He knew he'd never make it.

Zabetta took aim at a waspito hive dangling right beside Figley. She pulled back the flaming arrow and released it with a twang. The arrow pierced the hive, setting the papery walls on fire. Six glimmering waspitoes shot out to escape the smoke. They headed straight for the nearest target: Figley's furry bottom.

All six waspitoes buried their dart-tipped noses in his rump, and Figley screamed. He wrapped one arm around the vine and slid down as fast as he could, until he thumped headfirst on the ground. He yanked the waspitoes from his tush and scurried off toward Squonk Valley River.

When Figley reached the river, he jumped in.

He packed wet mud on his burning bottom, but it didn't help much. By the time he crawled back to his hut, his rear end had swelled up like a pudgie. He dragged himself onto his porch. All he wanted was to climb into bed and get some rest. Instead, he gagged on a horrible smell.

His hut was covered with swamp slime, a greasy, green liquid that stank like rotten mookling eggs. Shreds of snapping myrtle blossoms were scattered between the slime heaps. The petals added their sweet smell to the swampy stench.

"What happened?" Figley asked.

He didn't have to wait long for an answer. "Bombs away!" shouted a voice from the air. Figley looked up to see Rhumbler buzzing over his hut. She had stuck pollen in both nostrils to block the smell. A soggy bundle of swamp slime, wrapped in a pink snapping myrtle blossom, dangled from her arms. Rhumbler dropped the slime-bomb, and it exploded on his head. As she buzzed away, Rhumbler called over her shoulder in a cheerful voice, "Now we're even, Swamp Breath!"

Figley stumbled inside his hut. His eyes, ears,

and nostrils were filled with the rotten stink of swamp slime. He was too mad to cry. "Revenge," he growled. "I have to get revenge."

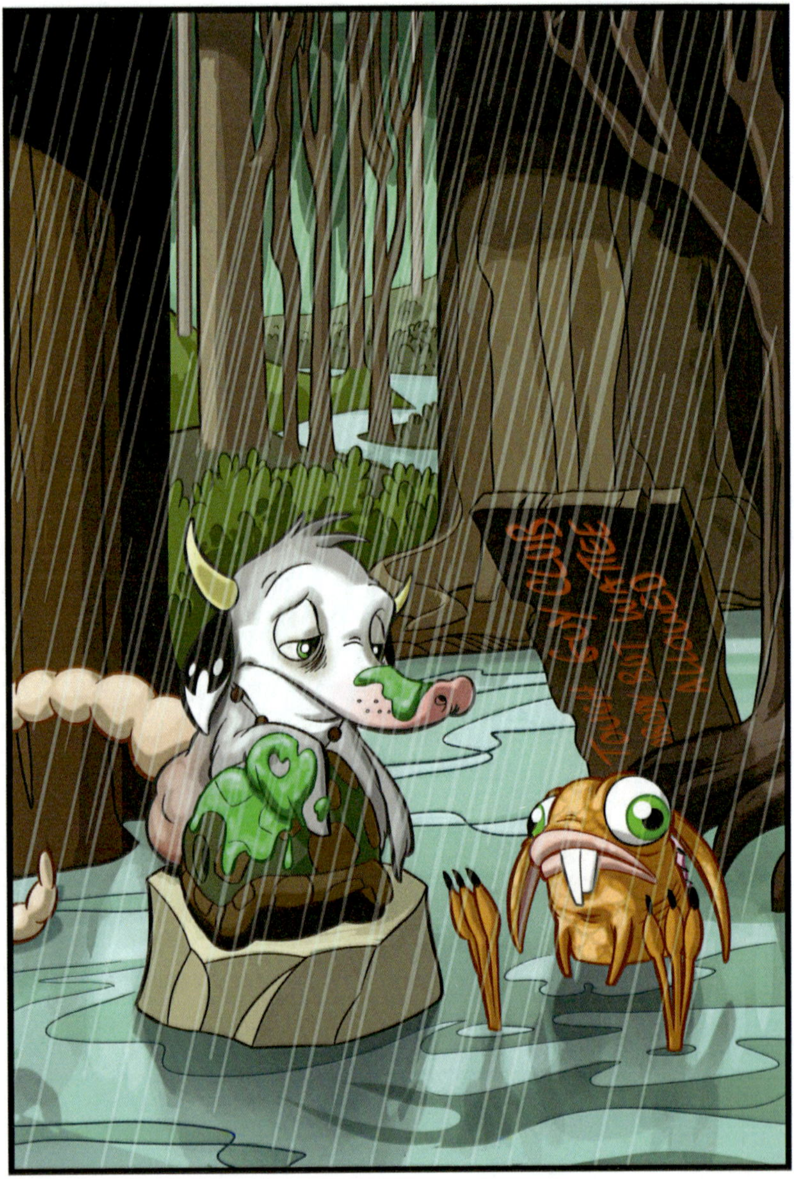

Chapter Four: War!

Figley found Wattee huddled on the muddy banks of Squonk Valley River. A light, warm rain had started to fall. Wattee had leaned an old board against the base of a tree to block the rain. The board said, "Tough Guy Club. Nobody But Wattee Allowed." Wattee stared at Figley's huge, swollen rump. He looked at the green swamp slime rubbed into his fur. A smile spread over his face.

"Zabetta wasn't too happy to see you, was she?" he asked.

"She set a bunch of waspitoes loose on me,"

Figley said. "And Rhumbler slime-bombed my house."

Wattee jumped to his feet and put his arm around Figley's shoulders. "You know what this means, right?"

"That I won't be able to sit down for a week?" Figley asked, rubbing his sore rump.

"Well, that too," Wattee said. "But it also means...WAR!"

It took Figley and Wattee an hour to clean all the swamp slime off Figley's house. It took them three more hours to build their secret weapon.

"It's amazing!" Wattee said. He leaned back to admire the huge crossbow they had built on top of Figley's roof. They had hacked a big curve of wood from a fallen tree to be the bow. They strung the bow with the droolly hammoth intestine from the slingshot. A pile of giant arrows was stacked on the roof. Each arrow was tipped with a hollow gourd, and the gourds were filled with the most disgusting things Wattee could think of—stenchaloupe juice, swamp slime, even some chunky drool they'd nervously collected from a sleeping droolly hammoth.

"Zabetta and Rhumbler will never know what hit them," Wattee said. He rubbed his hands together. "Let's see what they're up to." He stood up on the roof and shaded his eyes with one hand, looking across Tree Village to Zabetta's hut. "Oh, no, Figley!" he shouted. "Red alert! Come quick!"

Figley jumped to his feet. He looked where Wattee was pointing. Then he let out his breath in an "Oof" like he'd just been punched in the stomach.

Rhumbler and Zabetta had hammered together a platform above Zabetta's hut. They had built a huge catapult on top of the platform. The catapult's frame was built of bones and branches. The long wooden arm was tied to an eight-foot length of droolly hammoth intestine, with a gortuga shell at one end for loading ammo. Rhumbler buzzed back and forth from Zabetta's hut to the platform, carrying all kinds of things to load the catapult: waspito hives, stone jars, and a dozen rotten stenchaloupes Zabetta had found that afternoon.

"They're going to shoot us!" Wattee shouted. "How dare they? That's the meanest, nastiest trick I ever—"

"Umm, aren't we going to do the same thing to them?" Figley asked.

"Oh, yeah," Wattee said. He scratched his head. "And we'd better hurry. We have to get them before they get us!"

Smash! A waspito hive struck a house just below Figley's hut. Figley's neighbor, a little kid with floppy ears and a beak, ran out onto his porch. He howled in pain as he flapped his big ears at the cloud of waspitoes hovering above him.

Figley and Wattee ran to load the first arrow into their crossbow. "Fire!" Wattee yelled. They pulled the trigger, and the huge arrow flew into the air. The arrow missed Zabetta's hut, but it smashed into the next tree over. The gourd at the arrow's tip shattered against a tree, slopping swamp slime into the hammock that belonged to Zabetta's neighbor, an amphibious marsupial. The marsupial hopped out of her hammock and scooped the slime out of her pouch, shaking her fist at the sky.

A kind of madness took hold of Figley and Wattee then. They loaded each arrow as fast as they could, breathing hard. Figley's heart pounded in his chest, and the blood beat in his ears like thunder.

Crashes, smashes, howls, yowls, whacks, and thwacks cracked the peaceful night. There were some near misses. Figley leaped off the porch just before a rotten stenchaloupe would have thumped him on the head, and Rhumbler ducked an arrow that almost crushed her fuzzy belly. But most of the arrows and ammo missed their targets, creating havoc in Tree Village. Neighbors had fled their homes for the ground below, abandoning their huts as huge arrows flew through their windows and stenchaloupe splattered their doors.

Wattee and Figley loaded their last arrow into the crossbow and then stopped. An eerie silence had fallen.

"They must be out of ammo for their catapult!" Wattee squealed. He rubbed his hands together, grinning a crazy grin. "We won the war!"

Figley looked around at the broken branches and smashed huts. He listened to the wails and sobs from the frightened neighbors gathered below. Just an hour ago, this had been their peaceful neighborhood. "If this is what it feels like to win," he said softly, "I'd sure hate to lose."

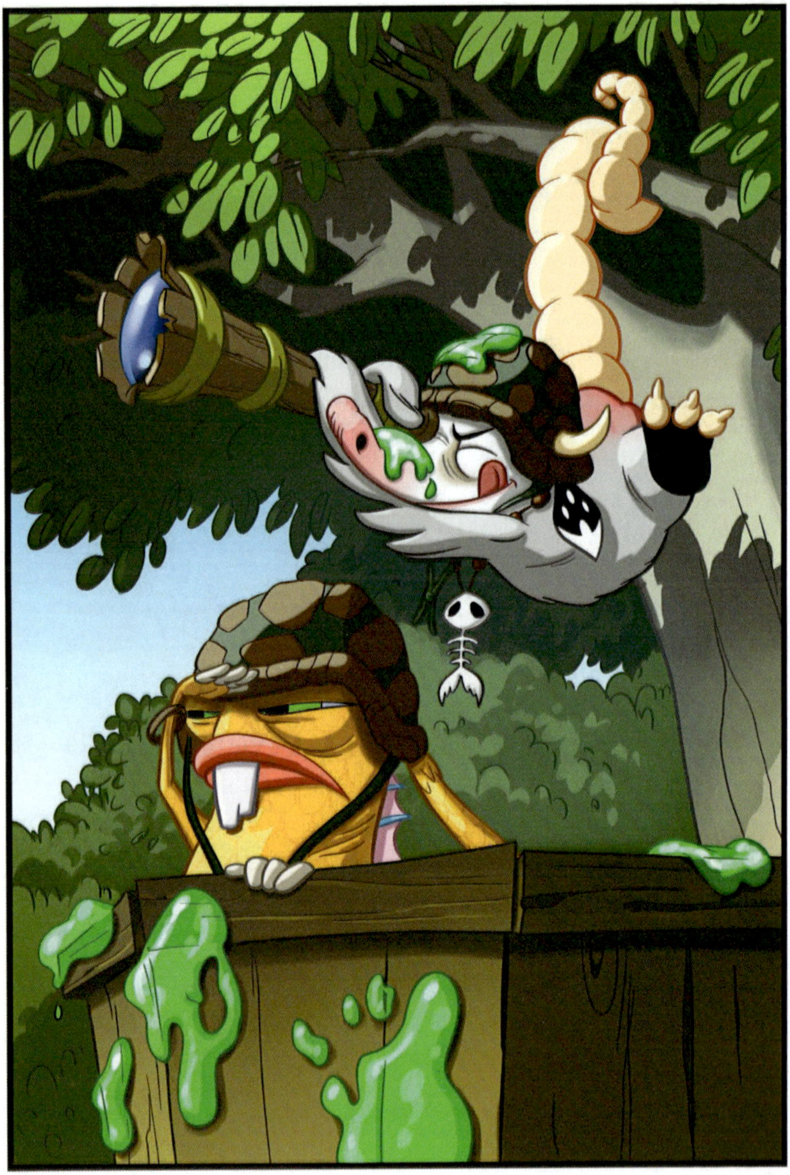

Chapter Five: Caught in the Crossfire

Figley looked over at Zabetta and Rhumbler. They were almost out of ammo, but not quite. Two rotten stenchaloupe melons sat on the porch, and one last waspito hive was loaded in the catapult. Zabetta and Rhumbler both looked as weary and worn out as Figley felt.

Wattee and Figley sat down to wait for whatever would happen next. Before long, they heard a scratching sound coming up the tree.

"It's them!" Wattee cried. "A sneak attack!"

Figley leaped to his feet. "We'd better get them before they get us," he said.

Wattee nodded. "Help me aim the bow."

They swiveled the heavy crossbow until it pointed straight down. They loaded the bow with their last arrow. The gourd at the arrow's tip was a Wattee's Special Triple Deluxe, filled with swamp slime, stenchaloupe juice, and hammoth drool. Figley squeezed the trigger, and their last arrow hurled down.

THUD-splash! "Owwww! Ewwww! Help!"

Wattee and Figley stared at each other, horrified.

"That sounded like—" Wattee gulped.

Figley finished his thought. "Chadwick! We'd better go help him."

They slid down a vine and found their friend Chadwick leaning against the base of a tree. His face was covered with swamp slime. His furry belly was stained with stenchaloupe juice, and hammoth drool oozed from both ears.

"Umm...hi, Chadwick," Wattee said.

Chadwick just stared at him. His spotted trunk curled, and he sniffed the greenish stenchaloupe clotted in his fur. "You shot me," he said. "Why?"

"Umm..." Figley looked at Wattee. Wattee looked back at Figley. "We didn't mean to. You just got in the middle of our war."

Chadwick stood up. He looked dizzy, and he swayed a little from side to side. "A swarm of waspitoes is flying around stinging everybody. Swamp slime is splattered everywhere, and the neighbors are all freaking out. What happened?"

Figley tried to explain. "It was this—well, it started when—umm, there was this song." He told Chadwick about the mean song Zabetta had been singing.

Chadwick held up one paw. "Wait a second. Did you hear Zabetta singing this song?"

"Yeah! I mean...not exactly," Figley told him. "But Wattee said that Rhumbler said that Zabetta said..."

"Uh-huh," said Chadwick. "That's what I thought." He lifted one of his webbed feet to wipe the hammoth drool off his toes. "Listen, Figley, Zabetta's one of the kindest Mutasians I know. And you're one of her best friends. I think you'd better go talk to her and find out what she really said."

"I tried that!" Figley wailed. He pointed at his oversized rump. "She sent a bunch of waspitoes after me. And Rhumbler swamp-slimed my house!"

Chadwick looked down at his swollen tush. "Zabetta did that? And Rhumbler...wait another second. Did you two do anything to them first?"

Figley pointed at Wattee. "You explain."

"Well, we started a club called 'The Tough Guys' Club,'" Wattee said. "You can join, Chadwick!"

Chadwick held up his paws. "Don't take this the wrong way, but I think I'd rather play spin-the-bottle with a snapping myrtle. What else?"

"Well, we kind of put a bunch of fishhooks all over the clubhouse. Zabetta might have stepped on one or two...well, six of them, I guess. And we maybe might have kind of...umm...shot Rhumbler in the teeth with nibs dipped in rotten stenchaloupe."

Chadwick closed his eyes and slapped himself in the face. "Still here," he muttered. He opened one eye to peer at Figley and Wattee. "I was hoping this was all a bad dream." He took a deep breath. "Listen, I'm going to go talk to Zabetta. If she'll agree to it, Figley, will you go talk to her?" Figley nodded. "Good," said Chadwick. "Wait half an hour, then go to your fishing rock in Squonk Valley River. It's time you two had a little peace talk."

Figley sighed. "I just hope she doesn't throw me in the river."

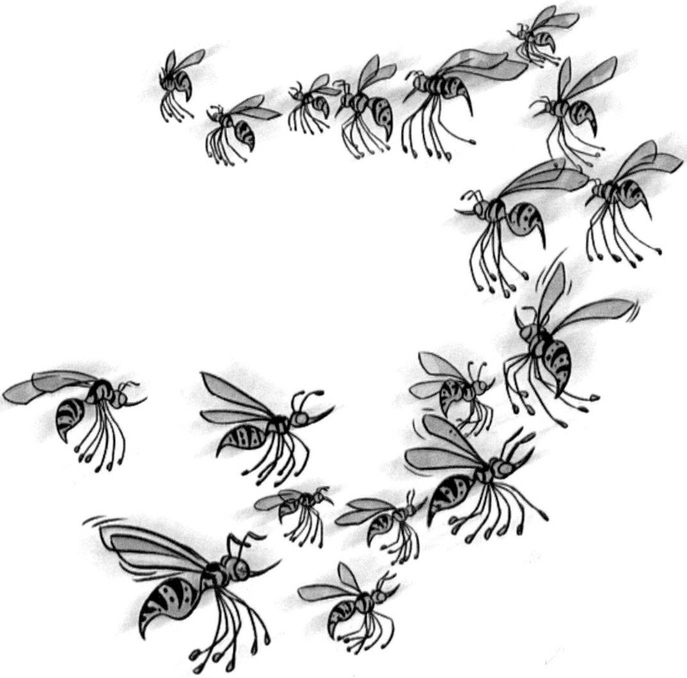

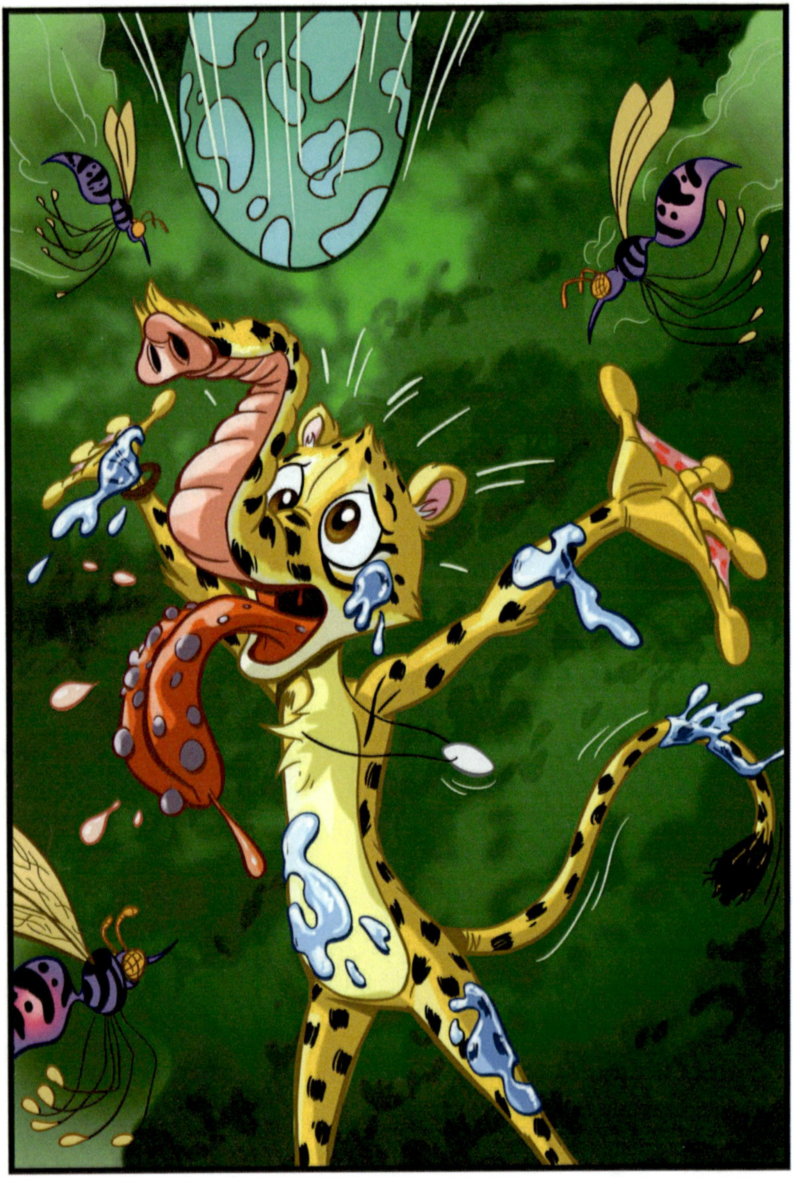

Chapter Six: Stung Tongue

Chadwick climbed the tree to Zabetta's hut. He was almost there when he heard an angry buzz. He looked up just in time to see a waspito nest flying toward him. The nest smashed on his head. Gray larvae oozed down his face. He licked off the larvae, smiling at the sweet, tangy taste. Then he froze. Tiny feet tickled his tongue like pinpricks. A bright purple waspito was walking back and forth on his tongue. It flexed its stinger first, then its pointy nose, trying to decide which one to use to sting him. Finally the waspito made up its mind and did both at once.

"OwooowoooowoooooooooOW!" Chadwick screamed. He jumped six feet in the air, flailing his webbed paws at the bark. He slid down the tree and fell flat on his back. When he got his breath back, he tried to scream again. His tongue was so swollen he could hardly get any sound out. His tongue was also covered in puckered blue spots, and the spots were inflating with pus like tiny balloons.

He staggered to his feet and started climbing the tree again. Rhumbler's voice floated down from the canopy above. "We got him! Fire again!"

Chadwick leaped out of the way just in time. A rotten stenchaloupe exploded on the tree behind him, spattering him with seeds and purple pulp.

He looked up and spotted a huge catapult made of wood and bone. Rhumbler was loading another melon into the gortuga shell at the end of the catapult's long wooden arm.

"Wait!" Chadwick shouted. It was hard to talk around his swollen tongue. "Don't thoot! I come in peath! It'th me, Chadwick!"

"Chadwick? Is it really you?" Zabetta called.

"I think tho," Chadwick said. "It'th a little hard to tell, becauthe I'm covered in thwamp thlime, hammoth drool, and rotten thtenchaloupe. My tongue hurth, too."

Zabetta slid down a vine. She carried her

spear in one hand. She also had a huge shield on her arm with painted letters that said "Fierce Females—No Boys Allowed!"

Chadwick read the sign and shook his head sadly. "I thought I wath your betht friend," he said.

"We didn't mean you," Rhumbler said. She buzzed down to join them. She wore a headband with the letters "FF" for "Fierce Females" painted on it. "We're having a war with Wattee and Figley. We thought you were one of them."

"I'm really sorry, Chadwick," Zabetta said. She stretched out a hand to help him up. "We didn't mean for you to get hurt. What can I do to make it up to you?"

"Talk to your friend Figley," Chadwick said. "He'th waiting for you right now down by Thkwonk Valley River."

Zabetta scowled. "No way," she said. "He might have been my friend this morning, but he's my enemy now."

"Then I'm leaving Tree Village," Chadwick said. He turned and walked away. "I don't want to live in a plathe where friendth are enemieth."

Zabetta took a deep breath. "Fine!" she said.

Chadwick pointed at her spear. "No weaponth."

Zabetta growled, but she turned and hurled her spear into the nearest tree. "Rhumbler, help Chadwick get cleaned up. I'm going to talk to Figley." She shook her head. "I just hope he ran out of swamp slime and hammoth drool."

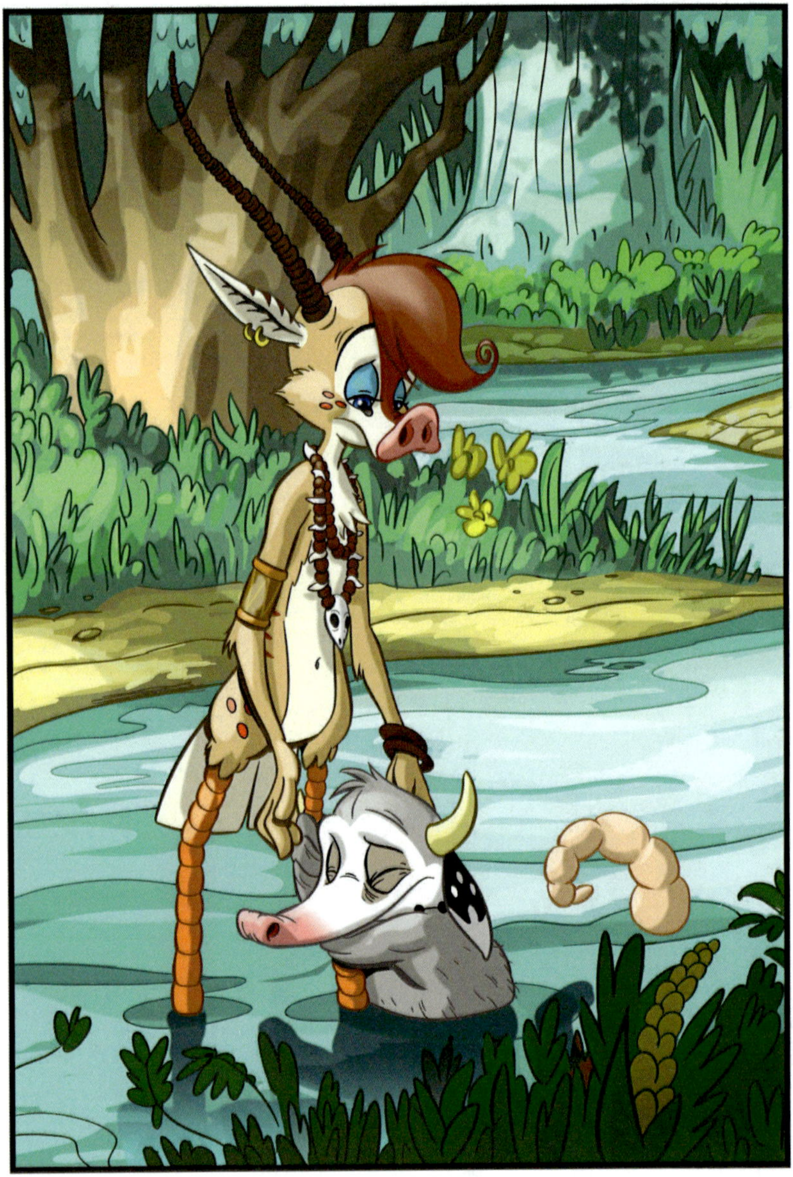

Chapter Seven: Peace Talk

Zabetta found Figley soaking his swollen rear end in Squonk Valley River. When he saw Zabetta, he scowled at her.

"So you came," he said.

"So I did."

They glared at each other. Suddenly, Figley burst into tears. Zabetta was so surprised, she just stared. Then she put her arm around her friend and patted his back. Ten seconds ago, she'd been boiling with anger. Now she just felt a lump in her throat that made it hard to talk.

"Why'd you sing all those mean things about me in that song?" Figley asked.

Zabetta stared at him. "What mean song?"

Figley took a deep breath and repeated the words: "Oh, Figley's my stinkiest buddy, he has such a goofy bald tail, he's fat and he's smelly, like stenchaloupe jelly, he's so weird we should put him in jail!"

Zabetta shook her head. "Are you crazy?" she asked. "That's not how the song goes! It goes like this. 'Oh, Figley's my jiggly buddy, he has such a squiggly tail, he's round and he's furry, and I never worry, because he's my number-one pal!'"

Figley stared at her. "You don't think my tail's goofy?" he asked.

"No!" Zabetta said.

"You don't think I'm smelly, like stenchaloupe jelly?"

"No way!" Zabetta said.

"And you don't think I'm fat?"

"No...umm..." She eyed his swollen rump. "Well, your bottom's a little chubby right now," she said. "But that's my fault, isn't it?"

Figley's eyes filled with tears. "Why did you attack me?" he asked.

"Because you attacked me first!" Zabetta said.

"That doesn't make it okay," Figley said. He rubbed his sore bottom.

"Yeah, well..." Zabetta took a deep breath and counted to ten. "You're right. I'm sorry, Figley. About all of it—Rhumbler slime-bombing your hut, and the waspito hives. And I'm sorry you thought I sang those mean things about you."

Figley wiped away his tears. "Thanks, Zabetta," he said. "I'm sorry about your foot. And your head. And Rhumbler's tummy. Are we still friends?" he asked.

"Yes!" Zabetta stuck out her hand and Figley

shook it. Then she gave him a big hug. "It's not too late for a half-birthday party," she said. "I have a few waspito larvae left. If you want to come over, I could make you a new cake."

Figley smiled. "Great," he said. "Wattee and I were so busy making weapons, we forgot to eat."

"Us too," Zabetta said. "We kind of lost our minds for a little while there. Crazy, huh?"

Figley nodded. "It was kind of a crazy day."

The two friends walked back to Tree Village. Zabetta's foot still hurt, and Figley's tush was still the size of a droolly hammoth's rump. But they were friends again, and that mattered more than everything else put together.

Epilogue: The Feast

The half-birthday feast was magnificent. Pots and pans simmered on tiny campfires built on Zabetta's roof. The smells of weeping onion, prickly potatoes, and droolly hammoth rump roast filled the air. Figley dangled by his tail from a branch above Zabetta's porch, stuffing larva cake into his mouth with both hands. Wattee was having a nib-spitting contest off the back porch with

Rhumbler. They were both laughing so hard the nibs kept hopping away before they got the chance to spit them. Zabetta stirred a bowl of hairberry punch with the handle of her spear. Chadwick kept plucking all the chunks of stenchaloupe out of the punch.

"I never want to see one of these again," Chadwick said. He tossed the soggy handful of stenchaloupe off the porch. "After all the chaos we've created, the neighbors probably want to chase us out of Tree Village. We'd better send them a pot of leftovers in the morning." He yawned and gently touched his healing tongue with one finger. "I need to get some sleep, Zabetta. I'll see you tomorrow."

Chadwick climbed down the tree, humming the song Zabetta had made up about Figley. It was a catchy tune, and pretty soon he started making up his own words.

"Oh, Figley and Zabetta acted crazy, with traps and mean weapons and more, but now that they're friendly, despite Figley's sore end-y, I'm off to my hammock to snore!"

Chadwick faded from sight in the shadowed branches below. Wattee and Rhumbler stared down at him, shaking their heads.

"Can you believe he said that?" Rhumbler asked.

"I know, right?" Wattee said. "What a mean song: 'Oh, Figley and Zabetta are lazy, with big mouths and green bottoms and more…'"

"No, no, no," Rhumbler said. "It went like this: 'Oh, Figley and Zabetta are zany, we should slap them and trap them and more, but now they're my enemies, I'll send them a…'"

"That's not it," Wattee said. "It was worse than that. He must've been really mad about that waspito sting. I think he said…"

The lights of Tree Village winked out like fireflies. Nibs scurried along the branches. Darkness settled on all the Mutasians in their beds, nests, and hammocks, bringing them a soothing night of peaceful slumber... for a little while, anyway.

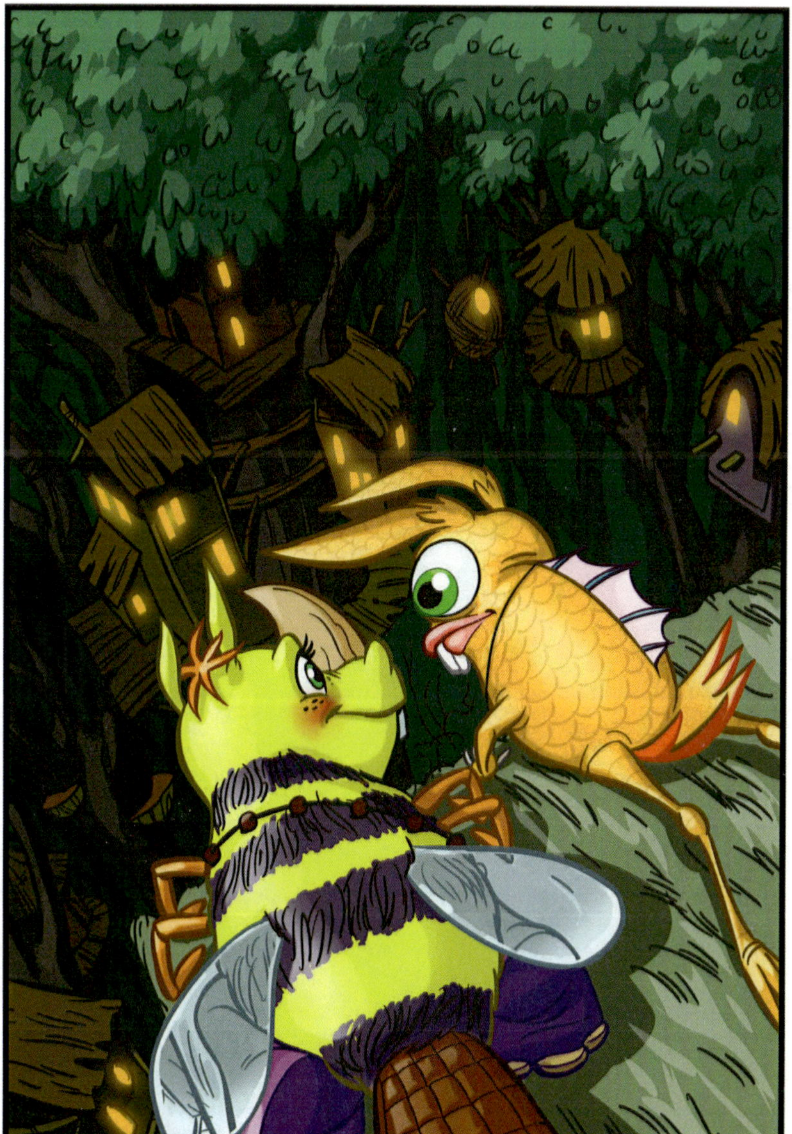

About the Author, Justin Minkel

Justin Minkel teaches 2nd and 3rd grade at Jones Elementary in northwest Arkansas. He has taught kindergarten through 7th grade in New York, California, Texas, and Senegal (West Africa), working with students who speak Spanish, Chinese, Marshallese, Wolof, Tibetan, and other languages. Justin is the 2007 Arkansas Teacher of the Year and National Teacher of the Year Finalist, a 2006 Milken Educator, and a member of the Teach For America 2000 corps. Justin is also a drummer, a hiker, a basketball player, and a dad to a son named Aidan and a daughter named Ariana. He recently completed a fantasy novel for students in the middle grades called *The First All-Children's Academy of Mallowmere*, which he hopes will be published in the near future.

Inspiration for "Clubhouse Clash"
The most important part of my students' day is recess, but that's also the time when most of their conflicts happen. It usually goes something like this: Katie runs up to me, her face red with fury, and says, "Maria doesn't want to be my friend anymore!" When I ask, "Did you *hear* her say that?" the usual answer is, "Umm, no, but Lauren said that Diana told her that Ruby heard...." I wondered how that game of "Telephone" might play out in Mutasia with Figley and Zabetta, and the result is the clash of the clubhouses that unfolds in this book.